A BOA

Before Mr. or Mrs. Hardy could tell them not to, Frank and Joe sprung from their seats, trying to get a closer look. They pushed through some of the crowd until they were only ten feet away from Sir Reginald and his wife. Sir Reginald set the briefcase down on the table, pointing inside to the spot where the pocket watch used to be. "It was here just four hours ago. And now it's gone!"

His wife put her head in her hands. Her eyes were so red, it looked like she was going to cry. "I don't know what happened," she said quietly.

A few waiters tried to calm Sir Reginald, but he shook them off, instead looking at the crowd that had formed around him. He stared at each person, his brows furrowed together, as if everyone were a suspect. "I know exactly what happened," he said. "Someone stole it!"

THE HARDY BOYS®

SECRET FILES #15

⚓ Ship of Secrets ⚓

BY FRANKLIN W. DIXON

ILLUSTRATED BY SCOTT BURROUGHS

ALADDIN ▪ NEW YORK LONDON TORONTO SYDNEY NEW DELHI

This book is a work of fiction. Any references to historical events, real people, or real places are used fictitiously. Other names, characters, places, and events are products of the author's imagination, and any resemblance to actual events or places or persons, living or dead, is entirely coincidental.

ALADDIN

An imprint of Simon & Schuster Children's Publishing Division
1230 Avenue of the Americas, New York, NY 10020
First Aladdin paperback edition August 2014
Text copyright © 2014 by Simon & Schuster, Inc.
Illustrations copyright © 2014 by Scott Burroughs
Series design by Lisa Vega
Cover design by Karina Granda
All rights reserved, including the right of reproduction in whole or in part in any form.
ALADDIN is a trademark of Simon & Schuster, Inc., and related logo is a registered trademark of Simon & Schuster, Inc.
THE HARDY BOYS is a registered trademark of Simon & Schuster, Inc.
For information about special discounts for bulk purchases, please contact Simon & Schuster Special Sales at 1-866-506-1949 or business@simonandschuster.com.
The Simon & Schuster Speakers Bureau can bring authors to your live event. For more information or to book an event contact the Simon & Schuster Speakers Bureau at 1-866-248-3049 or visit our website at www.simonspeakers.com.
The text of this book was set in Garamond.
Manufactured in the United States of America 0714 OFF
10 9 8 7 6 5 4 3 2 1
Library of Congress Control Number 2014939259
ISBN 978-1-4424-9045-1
ISBN 978-1-4424-9046-8 (eBook)

⚓ CONTENTS ⚓

Ship of Secrets

1

Ship Ahoy!

There it is! I can see it!" Joe yelled. He climbed over his older brother, Frank, who was sitting next to him in the taxi cab. He pointed out the window. Now that they'd turned into the harbor area, they could see the twelve-story cruise ship in the dock ahead of them.

"*Ship of Wonders*, here we come!" Frank cried.

Mr. Hardy, the boys' father, turned back from the passenger seat. "Your first cruise! You boys are going to love it."

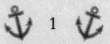

Mrs. Hardy held up a pamphlet that had a picture of the ship on the front. "There's a huge game room, a petting zoo, a trampoline, and magic shows and concerts at night. There are even seven pools—one for each wonder of the world."

"What are the wonders again?" Joe asked. They had gone over this three times before the trip, but he kept forgetting.

"Well, they're different depending on who you talk to," their mother said. The wind whipped through the windows of the tiny cab, blowing her thick brown hair into her face. "There are the ancient wonders of the world and the modern wonders. It looks like the ship has the modern wonders, which are different statues and monuments throughout the world."

"The Great Pyramid of Giza, the Great Wall of China, the Taj Mahal, and the Roman Colosseum are a few of them," Mr. Hardy explained.

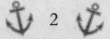

Mrs. Hardy leaned over, pointing out a few pictures from the cruise pamphlet. There was a circular building that had windows all around it. In the center was a huge pool. There were a few statues of men in armor standing near the entrance.

"The gladiators!" Frank exclaimed. As the cab pulled up at the curb, he drew an invisible sword, pretending to fight his brother. He swung once, then twice. Joe pulled out his own "sword," and the two jumped out of the cab, making clashing and clanking sounds as they fought.

"Careful!" Mrs. Hardy called out as she and their dad pulled the suitcases out of the trunk. They paid the taxi driver and followed behind the boys toward the huge ship.

Mr. Hardy rolled the suitcase behind him, letting out a big sigh. "One whole week of vacation. I've been waiting for this day forever."

Mrs. Hardy patted him on the back and smiled.

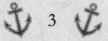

Joe and Frank's dad was a private detective in Bayport, their hometown. He worked long hours solving cases, sometimes robberies, other times more serious crimes. It seemed like he always had a file he was looking over or a lead he was "chasing down." (That was his detective way of saying "following a clue.") Frank and Joe didn't mind how much their dad worked, because he'd taught them how to solve cases. Together they

helped neighbors and friends find missing pets or property. Once they had to figure out who stole their science fair project, Mr. Roboto.

As they ran toward the ship, Frank and Joe still swung their invisible swords. Anyone looking at them wouldn't know they were brothers. Frank had dark brown hair and brown eyes, while Joe had moppy blond hair and blue eyes. Frank was an inch and a half taller than Joe. (But he was also a year older, Joe reminded people.) Joe raised his arm high in the air and was about to strike again, when he noticed a crowd at the end of the dock.

"What's going on?" he asked, pointing over Frank's shoulder. There were three news vans on the side of the road. Several reporters huddled around an older couple and their teenage children. The man wore a red scarf even though it was nearly ninety degrees. His puff of bright white hair made it look like a rabbit was sitting on his head.

"That man looks so familiar . . . ," Mrs. Hardy said. "I think I've seen him on the news."

"This has been in my family for more than a hundred and fifty years," the man said in a British accent. He held up a shiny gold pocket watch as he

spoke, moving it right in front of the news cameras. "It belonged to Duke Albert Heartpence III, my great-grandfather, who lived in England. And Monday morning, when this ship docks in Miami's harbor, it will be the center of Bartleby's Auction House's biggest auction yet."

The news reporters swarmed, some taking photos, others asking the man questions. One reporter asked how much it was worth, while others asked why he'd decided to auction it now.

"The time felt right," he said. He wrapped his arm around his wife as he spoke. Beside them the two teenagers looked uncomfortable in front of all the cameras. The girl looked to be several years older than Frank and Joe, with long brown hair braided down her back. The boy looked older, maybe seventeen, and kept checking his cell phone when his parents weren't looking.

"Who is that?" Frank asked, turning to his father.

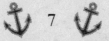

Mr. Hardy was staring at the scene at the end of the dock. "I read about this in the papers," he said. "I just forgot. That's Sir Reginald Heartpence II, some businessman from London. He's bringing that antique pocket watch to Miami to sell it in an auction."

"I hope those cameras aren't following him onto the boat," Mrs. Hardy said. They pushed past with their suitcases, walking toward the ramp that led to the ship's entrance.

But Joe and Frank were caught up in the excitement. They'd never seen so many news vans in one place. Cameras flashed, and people shouted out questions. Even as Sir Reginald and his family walked off toward the ship, the reporters followed.

"Is he a duke? Or a knight?" Frank asked his parents.

"Maybe he's a king!" Joe yelled.

"Definitely not a king," Mr. Hardy said, laughing.

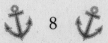 8

"Though he does act like one," Mrs. Hardy added, passing the suitcases off to a steward, who promised to bring them to their room.

"Can we go explore?" Frank asked as they stepped into the ship's glass elevator. Next to some of the top buttons were little signs. One said POOL LEVEL, another GAME ROOM, and another AQUARIUM.

"The pools!" Joe yelled. "We have to see those first!"

Joe and Frank hadn't been so excited since the first day of summer vacation. Their parents had been talking about this cruise for weeks, telling them about all the fun things there'd be to do on the ship. But when the elevator doors finally opened on the main deck, it was better than anything they could have imagined.

"The Great Wall of China!" Joe yelled, racing to a giant pool in front of them. There were slides

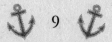

9

that looked like an old wall that went down into the water. There were already twenty or so people in the pool, splashing about.

"Look! There's the pyramid!" Frank cried out. There was a twenty-foot-high pyramid with a lazy river underneath it. A few boys went through a tunnel in bright blue inner tubes.

Joe ran around the deck, past some of the other pools they'd seen in the brochure. Real-life gladiators walked around the ship's deck, taking pictures with people. Frank drew his invisible sword again, but this time he pointed it at one of the men in costume. "This is going to be the best vacation ever!" he cried.

Joe followed his brother's lead, pretending to pull out his sword again. He couldn't stop laughing as they charged forward, toward the pool.

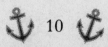

2

Watch Out!

The *Tyrannosaurus rex* opened its mouth and roared. Frank and Joe pulled more basketballs from the gutter and threw them into the hoop beside the dinosaur's head. "We are half-way there!" Frank yelled. "Keep going."

They grabbed another ball, then another, and tossed them into the hoop. Each one was painted white and purple, which was supposed to make them look like dinosaur eggs. The basketball hoop was shaped like a nest. The boys had discovered

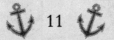

the game this afternoon, and they'd spent the last few hours inside the arcade, shooting hoop after hoop. Dino Ball (which is what it was called) had earned them more than fifty tickets. If they won fifty more, they could have their choice of prizes from the arcade.

"There you are!" Mrs. Hardy yelled across the crowded arcade. "We've been looking all over for you. This place is packed."

"Just . . . one . . . more!" Joe said. The timer ticked down. He tossed the last egg into the nest.

It went through, and the machine spit out ten more tickets.

"We're only forty tickets away from the grand prize, Mom," Frank said. He pointed to the wall across the arcade. There were stuffed toys of all shapes and sizes—bears, parrots, and even a giant banana. But Frank and Joe had their eye on the prizes on the very top shelf. There, above everything else, was a Soaker Shooter. It was one of the biggest water guns they'd ever seen.

"Seems like a scary game!" Mr. Hardy patted the giant dinosaur on the head. The *T. rex* was nearly as tall as he was, with scaly skin that looked real. The dinosaur showed them his shiny, plastic teeth.

"It's time for dinner, boys," Mrs. Hardy said. "You can win the rest of your tickets later. Promise." She waved them past a row of pinball machines, a photo booth, and a game where you hit gophers on the head with a hammer.

"Look what else we got." Joe held up a drawing of him and Frank together. It was drawn with thick black marker. They had huge heads and tiny bodies. They were each holding a magnifying glass, just like Sherlock Holmes would.

"Well, look at that!" Mr. Hardy laughed. "That's a nice picture of you two."

"He even drew a case file for us," Frank added, pointing to a folder he was holding in the picture. "Just like the kind you carry." They'd found the man on the main deck that day drawing pictures for anyone who wanted one. People would sit in a chair for a few minutes, and he'd look at them, then ask what they liked to do for fun. Sometimes he drew kids riding bicycles or playing soccer. Frank and Joe had told him how much they liked solving mysteries, so he'd drawn them like Sherlock Holmes. He called the pictures caricatures.

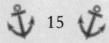 15

As they walked toward the main ballroom, they could hear the music starting. Inside there were hundreds of tables, all in front of a big stage. Most people were wearing nice dresses or button-down shirts. Some stood in line for food, while others ate dinner as they watched the show. Onstage a few dancers in red sequined gowns spun around in circles. A band played a loud song. The trumpets blasted out a few notes.

"What was your favorite part of today?" Mrs. Hardy asked as they sat down at their table. The plates were heaped with salad and breadsticks. Across from them was another family, with red-haired triplets who were about five. One of the girls was throwing crackers at her sister.

"The pyramid pool," Frank said. "No, no—I liked the game room the best. That dinosaur game is my favorite."

"What about the magic show? I loved how

the magician made all those cards disappear. I still don't know where they went!" Joe couldn't stop thinking about it. One minute there was a whole deck of cards, and the next minute they were gone.

Frank was going to mention the flamingo park on the top deck, or the clown who walked around the restaurant on stilts, but then the lights in the ballroom went down. A man in a tuxedo walked onto the stage just as the band finished their song. He had thick black hair and a mustache that curled up at the ends. "Ladies and gentlemen, welcome to the *Ship of Wonders*!" He waited until the crowd stopped clapping. "I'm Ricardo Ramboni, and I'll be your host for the next week, introducing some of the best musical acts you've ever seen. Tonight our first performers will be—"

There was a shriek somewhere in the crowd. Ricardo stopped talking. Every head in the room turned toward one of the front tables. "I don't believe this! No!" the woman cried. She pushed her chair back and lifted up the tablecloth.

"What's going on?" Frank whispered. "Who is that?"

Ricardo was still standing on the stage, frozen. He waved his hands, and someone turned on the ballroom lights. "Isn't that the woman from this morning?" Joe asked. "Sir Reginald's wife?"

The Hardy family watched as Sir Reginald Heartpence climbed out from under the table. His white hair stuck up in every direction. His cheeks were bright red, and his suit jacket was messed up. He held a small leather briefcase in his hand. "It's not here! It's not anywhere!" he yelled.

Ricardo stepped down from the stage, and a few waiters rushed in, trying to help the couple. Their teenage kids stood up, looking a little embarrassed. Every person in the ballroom was staring at them.

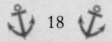 18

Before Mr. or Mrs. Hardy could tell them not to, Frank and Joe sprung from their seats, trying to get a closer look. They pushed through some of the crowd until they were only ten feet away from Sir Reginald and his wife. Sir Reginald set the briefcase down on the table, pointing inside

to the spot where the pocket watch used to be. "It was here just four hours ago. And now it's gone!"

His wife put her head in her hands. Her eyes were so red, it looked like she was going to cry. "I don't know what happened," she said quietly.

A few waiters tried to calm Sir Reginald, but he shook them off, instead looking at the crowd that had formed around him. He stared at each person, his brows furrowed together, as if everyone were a suspect. "I know exactly what happened," he said. "Someone stole it!"

3

The Case Begins . . .

Now, let's not jump to conclusions," Ricardo said, looking around. "Did you misplace it? Could it still be in your cabin?"

"Nonsense!" Sir Reginald yelled. "It was right here. Which one of you stole it? There's a thief among us!" He eyed the tables next to him. There were two four-year-olds coloring on the floor beside them. Sir Reginald glared at them, as if they might've crawled under the table and taken the pocket watch themselves.

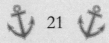

"Something tells me they're not suspects," Frank said, and laughed. The two kids could barely color in the lines. Opening a leather briefcase and stealing a watch would've been a pretty big challenge.

"You have to lock the doors," Mrs. Heartpence said, pointing at the ballroom doors on the other side of the room. Some of the crowd had finished their dinner and were now walking out, annoyed by the commotion. "The thief might be getting away!"

Mr. Hardy and Mrs. Hardy joined the small crowd. Mr. Hardy and the boys were already studying the scene like any good detectives would. They looked at the table and the tables around it, then kept an eye out for any suspicious people who seemed out of place. There were no signs that anything was off. Onstage the band started a new song, trying to entertain the guests who were still eating.

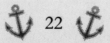

A man in a black suit came over with two security guards from the ship. "Sir, I am so sorry to hear about what happened, but let's discuss this somewhere else," the man said. Frank recognized him from earlier in the day. He was one of the cruise directors. He wandered around the ship, making sure everyone was having a good time. "We wouldn't want to spoil anyone's dinner, would we?"

"You cannot dock in Miami on Monday," Mrs. Heartpence said, ignoring him. "We can't. As soon as this ship is in the harbor, the thieves will smuggle the pocket watch off. They'll sell it as soon as they can. Then it will really be gone forever."

"I'm afraid we can't stop the ship's course," the director said. "Even for a valuable antique. Our security officers here will be on the case. Why don't you come to the employee's main office tomorrow morning and we will try to sort this out?"

 23

"Tomorrow?" Sir Reginald huffed. "You cannot be serious. Every minute counts. Why can't you see that?" His wife was practically in tears.

Frank and Joe looked at their dad. Mr. Hardy already had his notebook out and was scribbling notes. "Look, Dad," Joe said, pointing to the briefcase. "There's no lock on it. Did you write that down?"

"Fenton, you're supposed to be on vacation," Mrs. Hardy whispered. "No work, remember?" Mr. Hardy just smiled and shrugged.

The cruise director and the security guards left, and Ricardo went back onstage and told a few jokes to make the audience laugh. Within minutes it seemed everyone had forgotten about the watch. Everyone except Sir Reginald and Mrs. Heartpence.

"What are we going to do?" Mrs. Heartpence asked. "That watch has been in the family for years. And if we don't auction it—"

"Shhh," Sir Reginald said, holding up his hand. Whatever she'd been about to say, he didn't want her to mention it in front of everyone.

"It's okay, Dad," their son said. Their daughter had pulled her hair in front of her face. She looked embarrassed that her parents were still yelling about the pocket watch.

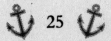

Mr. Hardy and the boys stepped forward. "Did you see anyone suspicious?" Joe asked, looking around at the nearby tables.

Sir Reginald shook his head. "No one that I can remember."

"I'm sure they'll be able to help you tomorrow," Mrs. Hardy said, looking at the couple. "Whoever took it couldn't have gone far." She shot Mr. Hardy a look that said, *Let's leave this up to someone else.*

But just then Mrs. Heartpence's eyes filled with tears. "I know I shouldn't say this, but I'm sorry, Reg. We need to find that watch. If we don't—" Her bottom lip trembled. She started to cry.

"What is it?" Mrs. Hardy asked. She held the woman's hand. Frank and Joe could tell their mother felt bad for her. Mrs. Heartpence seemed like she really did need their help.

"That watch belonged to Reg's great-grandfather,

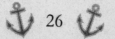 26

then his grandfather, then his father, and now us. And we need to auction it to help pay for our house . . . and Melinda's and Andrew's education. If we don't get it back, we'll be in serious trouble." At that, a few more tears fell down her cheeks.

Sir Reginald looked crushed. Frank and Joe knew then that it wasn't a question: They had to help the Heartpences find the watch. If they couldn't solve the case before the boat docked in the harbor on Monday morning, the watch might be gone forever.

"Please, Mom?" Frank whispered. "Can't we help them?"

Mrs. Hardy nodded, knowing it was the right thing to do.

Mr. Hardy offered Sir Reginald his hand to shake. "I'm Fenton Hardy, and I'm a private detective. These are my boys, Joe and Frank. We'll get working right away."

⚓ 27 ⚓

Sir Reginald looked at Joe and Frank, then at their dad. For the first time since the watch had gone missing, he smiled. "You'd do that for me?"

"Sure, we would," Frank said. "You just need to tell us where to start."

4

The Six Ws

Mr. Hardy looked around the giant ballroom. There was a security camera hanging in one corner. "See that? We might be able to find some clues on there," he said. "I'll go check with the ship's security people. Frank and Joe—you know what to do." He passed the boys his notebook and pen.

As his father headed out of the ballroom, Frank flipped to a clean page. Their father had taught them to start every case by listing the six Ws: Who, What,

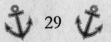

When, Where, Why, and How. They called this list the six *W*s, even though "How" didn't begin with the letter *W*. The What was the easiest part. *Antique pocket watch*, Frank wrote across the top of the paper.

"What exactly does the watch look like?" Joe asked. He knew it was good to have a very detailed description. That way they could tell the watch from any other one they might find.

"It's gold. There's a chain, and on the back the name 'Heartpence' is written in script," Mrs. Heartpence said.

Frank wrote down everything she said. "And when was the last time you saw it? Is there a reason you brought it to dinner tonight?"

"I told him not to," Mrs. Heartpence said, "but he was determined not to let it out of his sight."

"I made a mistake. . . ." Sir Reginald ran his hand through his thick white hair and frowned. "I saw it this afternoon. I was polishing it. I like to do that sometimes—give it a good polish. Then I put it right back into the case."

"About what time did you polish it?" Joe asked.

"Four o'clock," Sir Reginald's son said. "I remember because I'd just come back from the pool."

"That's right! Andrew had just come back from the pool, and Melinda was there with us, watching

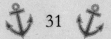 31

television," Mrs. Heartpence added. She pointed to their daughter, who was sitting, curling her long brown braid around her hand. She hadn't taken her eyes off the stage. A couple was salsa dancing. "Reginald and I stepped out for a snack at some point, but that was only for ten minutes or so. The kids were in and out of the room."

"It was nearly eight o'clock when we heard you shouting," Mrs. Hardy said.

"So the thief took the watch somewhere between four o'clock and eight o'clock," Joe added.

Sir Reginald nodded. "That's right."

Frank wrote "When" right below "What," and then put down the times. "So the pocket watch disappeared either from your room or from somewhere inside the ballroom."

"It was sitting right under the table by my feet!" Reginald said. "I had one foot resting next to it practically the whole time. Then, in the middle of dinner, I just had this funny feeling that I should check on it. Sure enough, it was gone."

Joe and his brother shared a look. It was hard to say exactly where the watch had disappeared from. It could have been stolen in the room, on the way to dinner, or in the ballroom. Frank decided to write down all three possibilities under "Where." They knew it was best to narrow the places down later.

Another dance ended, and some of the crowd got up from dinner, and left to go to other parts of the ship. Joe and Frank kept their eyes open for anyone who looked suspicious, but the ballroom was mostly filled with families. People watched the show, or picked desserts from the dessert table. There didn't seem to be a lot of suspects.

"Who could've done this?" Joe asked.

"Anyone!" Mrs. Heartpence said. "Anyone who wants to make a lot of money. The thief could be anywhere."

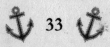

"But who was around during that time?" Joe asked. "You, Melinda, Andrew, and Sir Reginald were in the room. Was there anyone else you stopped to talk to along the way? Did anyone else come into the room after you polished the watch?"

"No," Sir Reginald said. "But now that you say that, I remember that I got into a fight with a steward this morning. He brought the wrong bag to our room. He was terrible! He had no clue what he was doing!"

Frank raised his eyebrows. "What happened?"

"I told him not to yell at the guy, but Reginald has such a temper," Mrs. Heartpence said. "And then the steward got angry and yelled right back."

"Where was the pocket watch when this happened?" Joe asked.

"In the room," Melinda said. She raised her head for the first time since Frank and Joe had started talking to her parents.

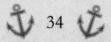 34

"He said 'You're going to pay for this' and 'You'll be sorry.' That seems like a threat, doesn't it?" Sir Reginald straightened his scarf. "Do you think he could've taken it?"

"Possibly," Joe said.

"We also saw my dad's friends Ollie and Margaret," Andrew added. "We ran into them on the way to dinner."

Mrs. Heartpence covered her mouth with her hand. "There's no way they would've stolen it. They're our close friends!"

Frank wrote down, *the steward, Ollie, and Margaret.* "It's good to have a complete list anyway. Maybe they saw something. You never know. Was there anyone else?"

"Not that I can think of," Sir Reginald said. "Those are the only people we talked to during that time. But now that you say it, I do think the steward had something to do with this. He was so

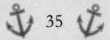 35

angry. And he could've come by our room when we stepped out. He could've taken it."

Joe scratched his head. There were hundreds of workers on the ship. How would they find this one guy? "What did he look like? Was he wearing a nametag?"

"Not that I remember," Mrs. Heartpence said. She patted down her stiff red curls, making sure her hair was perfect.

"He was young," Andrew said. "He had black hair and one earring. And really bushy eyebrows. His ears were kind of big, and I think he had a beard . . . one of those tiny ones."

"And blue eyes!" Sir Reginald added. "I remember that much."

Frank wrote down the description as fast as possible. They didn't have a name, but at least this was a good place to start.

"The motive seems easy," Joe said. He looked

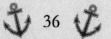 36

at his brother. "The watch is really expensive, and someone could sell it for a lot of money."

"It has to be the money," Sir Reginald said. "Why else would someone take it?"

"That's a good question," Frank said. He paced in front of the table. "We should try to think of other motives just in case. If the steward took it, it was probably because he was angry." Frank wrote down "revenge" under "Why." Still, it didn't seem like a steward would risk his job just because he was mad at Sir Reginald. There could be other motives too. It was just hard to know what they were.

"So, what do you think? Will you be able to find out who took the watch?" Mrs. Heartpence asked. She looked around the ballroom, which was emptying out. Then she dabbed at her eyes with a napkin.

"I hope so," Frank said. But as he looked down at the notes, he wasn't so sure. Joe shook his head, frustrated. Under "Who" they had only three people, and two of them were close friends with the Heartpences. Unless their dad could find out something from the security cameras, their only real suspect was the steward, and they didn't even have his name. The ship was filled with thousands of people and dozens of stewards. How could they possibly find this one steward in only two days?

5

The Mystery Man

The next morning Frank and Joe walked through the fifth floor of the giant ship. They looked at the two stewards carrying towels, then at the man wheeling a gold rack full of laundry. "Nope, nope, nope," Joe said as he studied the men's faces. None of the men looked like what Sir Reginald and his son had described.

Frank and Joe turned down another hallway, toward the indoor playground. Joe stared at the giant ball pit. Kids were jumping off a diving board

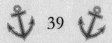

into it. Colorful balls flew everywhere. "That sure looks fun. . . ."

"We can't give up yet," Frank said quickly. "It doesn't matter how many stewards are on this ship. We only have two days to find our guy."

Joe knew his brother was right. He didn't want to give up, but so far they didn't have many clues. Mr. Hardy hadn't found anything on the security cameras from the ballroom. The cruise ship director had let him watch three hours of the tape, but it didn't seem like anything unusual had happened near the table. Mr. Hardy was going to spend the rest of the day looking at more tape from the cameras, while Frank and Joe tracked down leads. But their only real suspect wasn't anywhere to be found.

Frank walked past the playground and into the game room, where a few men in cruise ship T-shirts were standing. "Do you know a steward

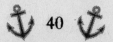

with an earring? Big ears? A tiny beard?" Frank asked them. The men all laughed and shook their heads.

The boys walked away, trying not to feel too discouraged. "It's hard to just tell people what he looks like," Joe tried. "It would be so much easier if we had a picture of him."

That's when Joe saw it. Off in the far corner of the game room was Max, the man who had drawn the picture of them just the day before. He had spiky hair and was mostly hidden behind a large easel. He sat on a stool, drawing on the easel in front of him. A little girl with brown pigtails was having her picture done.

"Are you thinking what I'm thinking?" Joe asked. "We could have Max draw a picture of our suspect. Didn't Dad say that's what he sometimes does when he doesn't have an actual photo?"

Frank smiled. "You're right!" He'd seen those

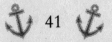

41

drawings on the news many times before. If they had a drawing of the man they were looking for, they'd be able to show it to people. It might not work, but it was worth a try.

When Max was done with the little girl's picture, they told him what had happened. "Do you think you could help us?" Joe asked.

"You betcha. Just tell me a few things about him." Max held his black marker in the air, waiting for them to give him the steward's description. Frank told him about the man's eyes and hair, and how he had a beard and big ears. Joe told him about the earring and bushy eyebrows. They tried to describe the man exactly how Andrew and Sir Reginald had.

"Maybe you could draw him in a steward's uniform too," Frank said.

Within minutes Max gave them a picture of their suspect. "This is perfect," Joe said. Max had

 42

drawn a more serious-looking picture than any of the ones they'd seen so far. The man had a weird expression on his face. He kind of looked like the type of person who might steal a pocket watch.

"Now we just have to find the real guy. Thanks!" Frank cried over his shoulder as they ran out the side doors. They scanned the hall, looking for the first steward they could find.

With the picture it took them only ten minutes to find someone who recognized their suspect. A waiter on the fourth floor said the guy's name was Ralph and that right now he was working as a gladiator at the Colosseum pool. "No wonder we couldn't find him," Joe said as they ran up the ship's stairs. "He was in disguise!"

When they got to the ship's back deck, they spotted two gladiators talking by the edge of the pool. They had silver helmets on that came down the sides of their faces. They each had plastic armor on their chest, and a shield strapped onto their arm.

Frank looked down at the picture, then up at the men. He looked back and forth, back and forth, until he was sure. "That's definitely him!"

he whispered, pointing at the guy on the left. He looked exactly like the picture. The only difference was his nose, which was much bigger in person.

As they walked toward the two men, Joe looked up at him. "Are you Ralph?" he asked.

Ralph nodded and smiled, but he looked a little confused. "Yes. . . . What can I do for you? Did you boys want your picture taken with two of Rome's fiercest gladiators?" He held up his sword. His friend, a shorter man with black hair, flexed his muscles.

"Actually, we wanted to talk to you about Sir Reginald Heartpence," Joe said. "We heard you two got into an argument yesterday in his room."

"I don't know what you're talking about," Ralph said. He'd stopped smiling as soon as he'd heard Sir Reginald's name.

"He said you brought bags to his room yesterday morning. Is that true?"

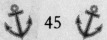 45

Ralph shifted on his feet. "Why do you ask?"

"Sir Reginald's antique pocket watch has been stolen. We're investigating what happened," Frank said. He studied Ralph's face as they spoke. His dad had taught them to always watch people's expressions. If the person's expression changed or seemed odd, it might be a sign that the person was lying.

"I didn't do anything, okay?" Ralph said. "I knew I was going to get blamed for this!"

"No one's blaming you," Frank said. This was always the trickiest part about questioning suspects—they would get angry if you thought they had something to do with the crime. "We're just trying to check every-one off our list.

Where were you yesterday between four o'clock and eight o'clock?"

"I'm tired of answering questions," Ralph repeated. His cheeks were bright red. Frank and Joe looked at each other. They could barely say a word without Ralph getting upset. Why was a simple question bothering him so much?

"Reginald said you told him you'd get back at him . . . that you wanted revenge. Is that true?"

"I only said that because I was angry!" Ralph said loudly. A few people lounging in pool chairs turned around, trying to see why he was yelling. "He yelled at me. All I did was bring the wrong suitcase to his room."

With that, Ralph took his helmet off and tossed it onto the ground. "I don't have to stand here and be questioned by you two," he huffed. Then without another word he stormed off.

Frank and Joe watched him leave. "He

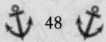 48

wouldn't answer any of our questions," Joe whispered under his breath. "What do you think it means?"

"He's hiding something," Frank said. "But what?"

6

A Secret Prank

Joe pulled out the notebook and began writing everything down. *First suspect leaves while being questioned,* he wrote. *Seems upset. Doesn't want to talk about where he was when the watch was stolen.*

Frank looked over Joe's shoulder. "We need to find Dad," he said. "Ralph wouldn't even talk to us. And now he knows he's on the list of suspects. If he did take the watch, we're giving him time to get rid of it."

"I know. It's all very suspicious. Where was

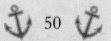

he yesterday? He doesn't have an alibi," Joe added. Their dad had taught them that word. No person could be in two places at the same time. If Ralph could prove he was somewhere else during the four hours when the watch was taken, Frank and Joe would know that he couldn't have stolen it.

They took off for their cabin, the notebook tucked in Joe's back pocket. "Wait!" a voice called out behind them.

Ralph's friend was running after them. He was much shorter than Ralph, and when he spoke, they noticed he had a gap between his two front teeth. "Don't go," he said. "Please don't tell the ship's security officers."

"What's wrong?" Frank asked.

"I shouldn't tell you this, but Ralph had nothing to do with that watch going missing."

"Then why wouldn't he talk to us?" Joe asked.

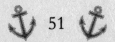

"We just wanted to know where he was yesterday afternoon."

"He was here, working with me. He was standing right by that deck," the man said, pointing to a podium on the other side of the pool. "You can check the schedules. He worked the pool with me from two in the afternoon until eight at night."

Joe was confused. "Why wouldn't he just say that, then?"

The man took off his helmet. He scratched his head like he was thinking about something. "This is the hard part. Can you keep a secret?"

Frank wasn't so sure. They were happy to keep secrets for friends, but they'd just met this man. They didn't even know his name! "We can try," he said.

"The thing is . . . Ralph sometimes plays pranks on the guests he doesn't like. This one time, he put a slug in a woman's hat. She was sitting right by the pool. He dropped the slimy thing into her hat and

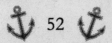 52

then just waited. Sure enough, a few minutes later she started screaming."

Joe couldn't help but laugh. He knew it wasn't right to play pranks like that, but it was kind of funny. "He did that?"

The man laughed. "Yup! And he's played other pranks too. Sometimes he'll put a bar of fake soap in the person's soap dish and it'll turn their hands blue. Anyway . . . he was planning a prank on Sir Reginald. And he asked around, wondering if he could get the key to Sir Reginald's cabin. He wanted to put cottage cheese in his shoes."

"So that's why he's worried?" Frank asked.

The man nodded. "Yup. He never got a key, but now he's scared everyone will think he stole the watch."

Joe wondered if the security guards had already heard about this. Did they know Ralph was a suspect? Had someone reported that he wanted the key to Sir Reginald's cabin? "More people might have questions for him," Joe said. "But he should try to tell them the truth. Otherwise he could be in big trouble."

"I know," the friend said. "I know. But believe

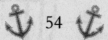

me, Ralph just wanted to scare Sir Reginald. He would never steal anything. He's just a big goofball."

Joe pulled out the notebook and added everything that Ralph's friend had said. "What's your name?" he asked.

"Paul Crowley." The man spelled it out. "And you won't tell our boss about the pranks, right?"

"We'll just tell him about Ralph's alibi," Joe said.

Paul smiled. "Well, I'd be happy to confirm where Ralph was yesterday. If you need me, I'll be right here." He put his helmet back on. Then he climbed back onto a podium at the edge of the pool, holding his shield in the air.

Frank and Joe kept looking at him as they walked away. "So Ralph was playing pranks," Frank said. "We'll have to check his alibi with the cruise director, but it doesn't seem like he did it after all."

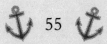

"No, it doesn't," Joe agreed. He flipped through the pages of his notebook. Then he drew a line through "the steward." Their one big lead had just become one big dead end.

Frank let out a sigh. There was only a day and a half left before the ship pulled into the harbor, and they weren't any closer to finding Sir Reginald's pocket watch. Frank kept thinking of how sad Mrs. Heartpence had looked when she'd found out it was missing. "Where do we go next?"

Joe looked at the only two names left on the list: Ollie and Margaret. "Just two last suspects . . . if we can even call them that."

Frank shook his head. "They're Sir Reginald's friends. I don't think we can." They walked off across the pool deck, darting around a giant statue of a horse and chariot. It was time for more questions!

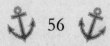

7

A Break in the Case

"The ship's security guards haven't found a single lead," Mr. Hardy said. "And those cameras aren't much help either. Most of the pictures are blurry. I'm proud of you boys for doing so much work."

"But, Dad, we barely have anything to go on!" Frank said. He pushed the notebook across the table. All that was written on the page was *Ollie* and *Margaret*. Two names. That was it.

"You ruled out Ralph as a suspect. That was

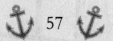

a big help," Mr. Hardy said. He took another sip from his coconut. They were sitting on the back deck of the ship, near a tropical-fruit stand. A man was selling pineapple slices and coconuts with straws stuck in their tops.

Just then a woman strode by, a tiny monkey on her shoulder. "Would you like a picture with

Mookey the monkey?" she asked. The little monkey stood up when she said his name.

Joe didn't even bother answering. He put his arm out and let the monkey walk right up it. The woman took a few pictures with her Polaroid camera, then handed them to him. The monkey was sitting on his shoulder when Ollie and Margaret finally showed up. "You must be Frank and Joe Hardy," Margaret said. She was tall and thin, with a white bun on top of her head.

She scrunched her nose at the monkey.

"And I'm Fenton Hardy," Mr. Hardy said. "Thanks for meeting us here." Ollie was a round man with tiny glasses. As they shook hands, Ollie and Margaret sat down.

"It's the least we could do," Margaret said. She seemed happier when the woman took the little monkey away. "We were so sorry to hear about Reg's pocket watch. It's been in his family for more than a century, you know."

"We do," Frank said. "That's why we need your help. When you saw Sir Reginald before dinner, did you notice anything unusual?"

Ollie put his hand on his chin. "He was carrying that leather briefcase, that's for sure. But he never opened it. I can't say if the watch was still inside or not."

Joe scribbled these answers down in the notebook. "What time do you think that was?"

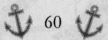

"Just before five," Margaret said. "Maybe a little earlier."

"And where were you?" Mr. Hardy asked.

"Right outside the ballroom. We were all going in for dinner when Reginald and I got to talking," Ollie said. "We were planning to play bridge this morning, but then the watch went missing."

"Did you notice anything odd?" Joe asked. "Was anyone suspicious standing around?"

"No, not that I remember," Ollie said. "It was very normal. Everything seemed fine."

Margaret nodded. "Nothing I can recall." Just then her cell phone rang and she turned away, talking loudly to someone about a fur coat.

"Are we done here?" Ollie didn't wait for them to answer. Instead he stood, reaching out his hand for Mr. Hardy to shake.

Frank frowned. "Is that it? You don't remember anything else?" he asked.

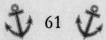 61

Margaret kept talking to the person on the other end of the phone, ignoring the Hardys. She was asking about the price of the coat when Ollie answered. "I'm sorry, I don't. I appreciate all you boys have been doing for Reg, but we're the last people you should be talking to. I own three islands in the Pacific Ocean. Why would I need an expensive pocket watch?"

Mr. Hardy stood. "We didn't think you took the watch," he said. "Just that you may have seen something."

Ollie laughed. "You shouldn't be questioning me. You should be questioning that girl from the game room. The one everyone's talking about."

Frank and Joe looked at each other, confused. "What girl?" Frank asked. This was the first time they'd heard about her.

"Some kids in the game room saw a girl last night with the watch," Ollie said. "You didn't hear?

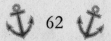

A bunch of them have been talking about it. We were stuck in the elevator with them while they went on about it. I thought everyone knew."

"What time was it when the kids saw her?" Frank asked.

Ollie shrugged. "I'm not sure. I just know that it was last night."

Without saying another word he and his wife strode across the deck, leaving Mr. Hardy and the boys behind. "Finally! A break in the case!" Joe said. He was so excited, he was nearly yelling.

But Mr. Hardy was worried. "Someone in the game room was spotted with the watch," he said. "But who? I'm going to check the cameras one last time. You boys see if you can find the kids that Ollie was talking about. There must be witnesses."

Mr. Hardy went toward the pyramid pool, and Frank and Joe headed in the opposite direction, down to the game room. "This is the best news

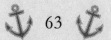

we've had all day," Joe said. "I only wish we'd heard it sooner."

But Frank didn't mind. He loved when a case suddenly changed and new information was discovered. Their dad always said "breaks" were the most fun part of the job. As they went down the stairs, Frank couldn't run fast enough. "Hurry!" he said. "We need to find that girl with the watch!"

8

Red Scarf Sighting

When they got to the game room, it was packed with kids. There was a group standing by the pin-ball machines watching a girl break the high score. Two boys were playing a race car game. Joe looked to the corner of the room, where a set of brown-haired twins shot basketballs for Dino Ball. Even now Joe was still thinking of the Soaker Shooter and the forty tickets they needed to get it.

"Where should we start?" Joe asked, looking around. Two boys ran past, chasing each other.

"You go that way," Frank said, pointing toward the ringtoss. "And I'll go this way." Then he took off.

Frank moved through the crowd, stopping at a girl with a hammer. She was watching a bunch of holes, waiting for little plastic gophers to pop up so she could hit them back down. "Can I ask you a few questions?" Frank said.

The girl bit her lip, then hit a gopher on the head. "Sure."

"I heard a rumor that there was a girl here last night. A few kids saw her with a pocket watch."

The girl smashed one of the gophers down, and the machine spit out a whole line of tickets. "I didn't see her," she said.

"Do you know anyone who did?"

Before Frank could say another word, he heard Joe calling him from somewhere across the room. "Frank! I found them! Frank!"

Frank darted through the crowd. Joe stood with two girls and a boy. They were leaning against a dancing game. Another boy was stepping on

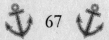

different-colored pads and moving his arms in the air. "Dance to the music," an electronic voice said over and over again.

"I saw her last night, around five," one of the girls said. "She stood out because she had a red scarf around her head."

"And sunglasses!" the boy, who had freckles, added. "Don't forget the sunglasses."

Joe scribbled everything down in his notebook. "What color hair did she have?"

"Brown," the boy with freckles said.

"No, she didn't," the second girl argued. "She had blond hair. And she wore a long tan coat."

"I thought the coat was gray," the boy said.

Joe wrote down *Hair: brown or blond*, then *Coat: tan or gray*. This was sometimes a problem with witnesses. They disagreed about what they had seen. "Everyone thinks she had a red scarf, though?" Joe asked.

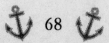

"Yes!" the three kids shouted at once.

"And was she carrying the pocket watch when you saw her at five?" Frank asked.

The second girl, who wore glasses, nodded. "When she came in, I saw the watch in her hand. I thought it was odd, but then I went back to playing pinball. I was in the middle of a game and close to beating my high score."

"Did she have it when she left?" Joe asked.

"Nope. She left only a few minutes later, and it was gone."

Frank looked at his brother. "She might've hidden it here," he said.

"Or given it to someone," Joe added. He looked at the kids. "Did you see her talking to anyone?"

"Nope," the freckled boy said. "But I was busy playing Hungry Alligators." He pointed to a game by the door. On the screen, alligators were chasing a swimmer down a river.

⚓ 69 ⚓

"We couldn't really tell what she looked like," the girl with glasses added.

"How old?" Frank asked.

"Not sure."

Frank was about to ask the girl for another description of the girl's scarf, but then his father walked through the door. He was holding a sheet of paper in his hand.

"I've been looking for you two!" he called out.

When he got closer, Frank and Joe saw what it was. It was a picture of the girl the kids had described. "I spent the last hour going through the video footage from the game room," he said. He pointed to a camera in the corner. "That camera caught our suspect coming in the door with the watch, and leaving without it. Security helped me print these out."

Joe looked at the picture. It was blurry, but you could see the pocket watch in her hand as she walked in. Then, in the next photo, her hands were empty. "Is this the girl you saw?" Joe asked the kids they'd been talking to.

"That's her! Definitely," the boy said.

"And she didn't talk to anyone while she was here?" Frank asked again.

"I really don't think she did," the girl without the glasses added. "I looked at her a few times. She was always alone."

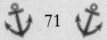 71

"It seemed like she was looking for something," the boy said. "She went around to a couple of the games, but she didn't play any."

Mr. Hardy put his hand on his sons' shoulders. "It's possible she came here to find a safe spot to put the watch until the ship pulls into the harbor. If she stole it, it might've been too risky to carry it around or keep it in her room."

"It's Saturday night, and the game room is closing in fifteen minutes," Frank said. "The ship pulls into Miami at eight a.m. on Monday morning."

"Which means . . . ," Joe said. "She'll be back at some point tomorrow to get it."

Frank and Joe looked around the game room, which was emptying out. A man in a cruise T-shirt was sweeping popcorn off the floor. "Are you thinking what I'm thinking?" Frank asked. He pointed to the photo booth in the corner. There

 72

was a curtain covering the inside. Taped to the front of it was a sign that said OUT OF ORDER.

"Stakeout?" Joe asked.

"Stakeout," Frank said, smiling.

Mr. Hardy nodded. "Great idea, boys. It'll be impossible to find the watch in here without some help. When she comes back tomorrow, she'll lead you right to it."

Joe felt more hopeful than he had all day. Tomorrow they'd be on a real stakeout, just like in the movies. With a little luck they'd get the watch back to Sir Reginald by nighttime.

"What are you going to do?" the boy with the freckles asked. He looked confused.

"We're going to do the easiest thing," Joe replied. "Tomorrow we're going to sit in that booth and just wait."

9

Straight from the Dino's Mouth

Joe pushed his feet against the wall, trying to get comfortable. "I can't feel my legs," he said. He folded himself in half and tried to squeeze into the corner.

"Join the club," Frank said, and laughed. Joe could barely hear him, though. Frank was poking his head out from behind the booth's curtain, looking for the girl from the photo.

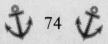

There was popcorn and empty juice boxes on the photo booth floor. Their mother had packed them lunch, including turkey sandwiches from the ship's dining hall. They'd been stuffed into the booth for more than five hours now, but there'd been no sign of the girl. "She has to come back," Joe said. "Doesn't she?"

"I hope," Frank said. But it was feeling less likely. It was almost two o'clock. Half the day had passed, and they still hadn't seen her.

Frank drew the curtain closed again. "Your turn," he said, climbing over his brother. They switched spots, so Joe was sitting on the outside. They'd done this all day, taking turns keeping watch.

Joe pulled the curtain back just an inch so that he had a good view of the game room. Because it was Sunday, it was busier than ever. A group of kids

was standing around the dancing game, watching a girl who was really good. She jumped and kicked in time with the music. They all cheered when she beat her high score.

Ten minutes passed, and Joe was so busy watching the scoreboard that he almost didn't notice the girl walk in. She had the same red scarf on that she wore in the picture. Her sunglasses were so big, they covered half her face. "Psssst! Frank!" Joe whispered. He nudged his brother in the side. "I see her! She's here!"

Frank sat up straight. "It's about time!"

They both squeezed into the front of the photo booth, looking out into the game room. The girl wore a long gray trench coat and had brown hair, just like the boy had said. She looked around as if she knew someone was watching her. Then she took off toward the other side of the room.

"We have to follow her," Joe said. He stepped out of hiding. He and Frank crept along the wall, trying to stay out of sight. They watched the girl move through the game room. She went past the pinball machines and the Hungry Alligator game.

 77

When she stopped, they stopped, hiding themselves behind a bouncy castle.

"She's going to Dino Ball!" Frank said. He
couldn't believe it. She walked right up to the
game and stood there, watching two boys shooting the dinosaur eggs into the nest. "What does
she want with that game?"

"Shhhh," Joe whispered. "Just watch." He didn't mean to be rude, but Frank was always talking on stakeouts. The last time they'd been watching a thief, he'd nearly blown their cover. (That was what their dad called it when people discovered you were there.)

The girl stood still. The two boys kept shooting basketballs into the nest. Then she looked around, and without saying anything to anyone, she reached her hand into the *T. rex*'s mouth. When she pulled her hand out, she was holding something. "The watch! It's the watch!" Frank whispered.

Joe put his hand over his brother's mouth to keep him quiet. They studied the girl. She turned the gold watch over, making sure it was okay. Then she looked around to make sure the boys hadn't noticed her—they were too busy shooting basketballs to really notice—and she headed for the door. "We have to do something," Joe said. "She's getting away!"

Frank sprung out from behind the castle. "Stop! Wait right there!" he yelled.

The girl turned around. Then she tucked the watch into her pocket and ran as fast as she could in the other direction. Joe and Frank followed her. A chase was on!

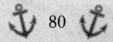

She ran down a staircase that led into the grand ballroom. Onstage a man with long hair was singing Broadway show tunes. He kicked high in the air as he belted out a few last notes. Couples were dancing to the music.

The girl darted between the dancers, nearly knocking some of them over. "Hey! Watch it!" an old man yelled. "You nearly toppled me to the ground!"

Frank and Joe never took their eyes off her. They were only ten feet behind her, and they tried to keep up. But she was fast. A little *too* fast.

"I don't know if I can keep running!" Frank yelled to his brother as they ran up another set of stairs. "I can barely keep up!"

Joe and Frank followed their suspect through another hallway, then a room with card tables. People were playing poker and rummy. A dealer pushed plastic chips around on a table. "You're

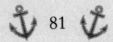 81

right," Joe said. "And she definitely isn't an old lady!" The scarf and trench coat looked too big, like they had been borrowed from someone else.

The girl ran out of the card room and down another hall. The boys sprinted as fast as they could. "Hurry!" Frank yelled. "She's getting away!"

She turned right, and they turned right. She turned left, and they turned left. She kept running through the maze of hallways, but they kept right behind her, not slowing down. Joe was nearly out of breath. Just when he felt like he couldn't go any farther, she took a left . . . and the hallway ended. Their suspect was cornered!

"All right! All right!" the suspect yelled. "You caught me. I'm sorry."

Frank and Joe stood in the hallway, trying to block her exit. But she didn't try to run. Slowly she undid her red scarf, letting her dark hair fall

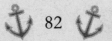 82

down around her shoulders. Then she pulled off her sunglasses. Standing in front of them was Sir Reginald Heartpence's own daughter. She took the pocket watch from her coat and held it in her hand.

"Please," she said, her eyes filling with tears. "Let me explain."

10

The Confession

Frank and Joe just stood there, shocked. They had never suspected that Sir Reginald's daughter had anything to do with the case. She'd just sat there listening when the boys had questioned her parents. They'd had no idea that she was the thief!

"Melinda?" Frank asked. He could barely remember her name. "Why would you steal your dad's watch? We've been looking all over for it. Your parents were so upset."

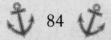 84

"I'm upset!" she said, tears on her cheeks. "This isn't my father's watch. This is my grandfather's watch. It was his, and now my dad is selling it."

"But your parents said they have to," Joe tried to explain.

Melinda shook her head. "I don't care. I don't want them to. . . . I was so close to my grandpa before he died. He called me Little Lindy. And he always carried this watch around. It's been in our family forever. If they sell it, what do I have to remember him by?"

Frank lowered his head. He felt a little bad for Melinda now. He could tell the watch meant something to her, and she was very upset her parents were selling it. But she still shouldn't have taken it without asking. "You could've told your parents how you felt," he said.

"They wouldn't have listened," Melinda said. "They never listen."

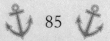

"So you just took it?" Frank asked.

"When they left the room Friday afternoon, I took it from the case. Then when they were talking to Ollie and Margaret, I told them I needed something in the room. I used that time to get dressed, go down to the game room, and hide it. I know how crazy it must seem, but I didn't know what else to do," Melinda said.

"Well, I'm sure they'll be happy to see it again," Joe said. "Why don't we all go to your parents' cabin and talk about this? We know you're upset, but your parents are upset too. You need to tell them the truth."

Melinda bit her lip. Her eyes filled with tears again. "I don't want to," she said. She wiped her cheeks off as she spoke.

"I think there is something you need to give back," Frank said. He held out his hand. "We'll help you."

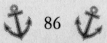 86

Slowly, without saying a word, she gave the watch to Frank. Then she followed them up the stairs to the family's cabin, where her parents were waiting to hear news of the stakeout.

"Melinda dear," Mrs. Heartpence said. "We just wish you would've told us you were upset. We had no idea."

She and Sir Reginald sat on the couch in their cabin. Mrs. Heartpence held her daughter's hand.

"I wanted to, but I didn't know how," Melinda said.

Her brother, Andrew, just shook his head. "We've had the whole ship looking for that watch! I can't believe you did this, Mel."

"It's all right," Mr. Hardy said. He stood beside Mrs. Hardy and the boys, looking on. "We were all happy to help. We're just glad we found it."

"Melinda, we don't want to get rid of the watch

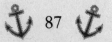

either, but we have to. It'll help pay for the house, and for your and Andrew's college education. Your grandfather would've wanted to help us do that," Sir Reginald added.

"But if we sell it, I won't have anything to remember him by," Melinda said sadly.

"That's the thing, though," Mrs. Heartpence replied. "We'll have our memories of him. And pictures. Remember that time he took you to the zoo? You were in love with the bears, and he sat there with you for hours, just watching them. He loved being around you."

"Or the time he brought you to the sweetshop in the city?" Sir Reginald continued. "You two had frozen hot chocolate. You talked about that for months afterward. You had the greatest time."

Melinda sniffed back tears. She smiled at the memory. "That was the best day."

"See, dear?" Mrs. Heartpence said. "It doesn't

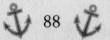

matter if we have the watch or not. Your grand-father will always be with us. We think about him all the time. How could we not?"

Sir Reginald gave his daughter a big hug. For the first time Joe noticed that the red scarf Melinda had worn as a disguise was Sir Reginald's scarf. It was the same one he'd worn the first day of the cruise.

Then Sir Reginald turned away and stood up from the couch. He clapped Frank and Joe on their backs. "You boys did an amazing job," he said. "If it weren't for you, we never would've talked about this. We might not have found the watch at all. I can't thank you enough."

"We're happy we solved the case," Joe said. "And the watch is back to its rightful owner."

Frank and Joe turned to leave, their parents right behind them. Before they could reach the door, Sir Reginald called out to them, "Tomor-row, when we pull into the harbor, I'd like you to be my special guests at the auction. They'll be a huge party afterward. A giant feast with music and dancing! Will you join us?"

Mr. Hardy looked at the boys. Frank and Joe smiled. A party sounded like the perfect reward for their hard work.

The band played a fast song, and Frank and Joe danced on the open roof deck. From the top of the tallest building in Miami, they could see the entire harbor, including the giant cruise ship.

"This has been the best part of the trip so far!" Frank exclaimed. Across the dance floor his mom and dad swung each other around. They were really getting into the music.

"My favorite part was the chocolate fountain," Joe said. They'd spent more than an hour dipping strawberries and marshmallows into it. Joe still had chocolate around his top lip.

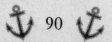 90

Frank was about to say something about the coconut cake, or the giant stack of lemon candies that were piled high on the dessert table, but then Melinda came over to them. The party was ending. Mr. Hardy waved at them to get their coats.

"Thank you guys again," Melinda said. "You

were right. I should've just told my parents what was wrong."

"No problem," Joe said. "We had fun on our stakeout. You were a tough thief to catch!"

Melinda's cheeks turned bright red. "Well, I'm glad you caught me. I might've never told my parents. I was so scared once I'd taken the watch. I didn't even know what to do with it!"

Across the room Sir Reginald chatted loudly with his friends. He held his wife's hand. He looked happier than he had all weekend. Frank looked at him, then back at Melinda. "That was one place your dad would never have found it. The *T. rex*'s mouth!"

Joe, Frank, and Melinda all laughed. "Is that game any good?" Melinda asked.

"Good? It's the best game on the ship!" Frank said. "It's called Dino Ball. We'll teach you some-time."

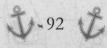

"How about now?" Melinda laughed. "I could use some friends. My parents decided not to punish me . . . at least not yet. This might be my last night of freedom."

Joe smiled. "Well, come on, then!" he said. "Let's go back to the ship. Dino Ball is waiting . . . and so is our Soaker Shooter."

"What's a Soaker Shooter?" Melinda asked.

"We'll explain later," Frank said. He looked at his brother. Now they could enjoy the rest of their vacation. They couldn't wait!

SECRET FILES CASE #15: SOLVED!

TEST YOUR SLEUTHING SKILLS

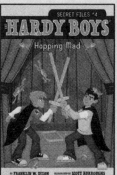

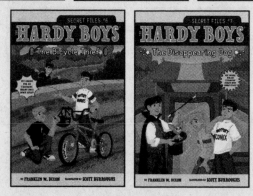

WITH THESE OTHER CASES!

Nancy Drew and The Clue Crew®
Test your detective skills with more Clue Crew cases!

FROM ALADDIN • PUBLISHED BY SIMON & SCHUSTER

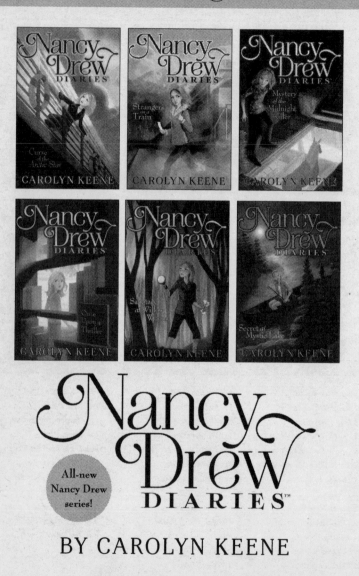

Join Zeus and his friends as they set off on the adventure of a lifetime.